Christmas Joy!

A celebration of the holiday spirit in poetry, photography, and music

Poems selected by Julie Aigner-Clark

Illustrations by Nadeem Zaidi

Hyperion Books for Children
New York

For information address Hyperion Books for Children, 114 Fifth Avenue, New York, New York 10011-5690.

Printed in Singapore

ISBN 0-7868-0804-7

Library of Congress Cataloging-in-Publication Data on file.

Visit www.hyperionchildrensbooks.com and www.babyeinstein.com

Grateful acknowledgment is made to the following for permission to reprint the material listed below:

The lines from "little tree": Copyright 1925, 1953, © 1991 by the Trustees for the E. E. Cummings Trust.
Copyright © 1976 by George James Firmage, from Complete Poems: 1904–1962 by E. E. Cummings, edited by George J. Firmage.
Used by permission of Liveright Publishing Corporation.

"Snowflakes": From Around and About by Marchette Chute, copyright 1957 by E. P. Dutton.
Copyright renewed 1985 by Marchette Chute. Reprinted by permission of Elizabeth Hauser.

Photo credits: Boy Eating Snowflakes in Winter © Andre Gallant / The Image Bank; Snowy Pine Tree on Hill with Winter Forest © John P. Kelly / The Image Bank;
Close-up of a Fire in a Fireplace © Martial Colomb / Photodisk; Snowflakes © W. Perry Conway / CORBIS; Girl with Present © Ross Whitaker / The Image Bank;
Lori & Scott in Horse Drawn Sleigh in Aspen, Colorado © John P. Kelly / The Image Bank; Japanese Bells © Daisuke Morita / Photodisk;
Holly Leaves and Berries in Snow © Andrew Ward / Life File / Photodisk; Icicles © Jeremy Hoare / Life File / Photodisk;
Christmas Stocking on a Fireplace © Malcolm Piers / The Image Bank; Santa Looking Through Frosty Window © Per-Eric Berglund / The Image Bank;
Apple Orchard in Winter, Washington, USA © Steve Satushek / The Image Bank; Boy with Reindeer Puppet © Ross Whitaker / The Image Bank;
Snow-Covered Barn and Trees—Illinois © Willard Clay / FPG International; Northern Cardinal Perched on Branch © Gary W. Carter / CORBIS;
Sleeping Arctic Fox © PhotoLink / Photodisk

Snowflakes
dance like children,
equally beautiful,
beautifully unique.

—Julie Aigner-Clark

little tree
little silent Christmas tree
you are so little
you are more like a flower

who found you in the green forest
and were you very sorry to come away?
see   i will comfort you
because you smell so sweetly . . .

and my little sister and i will take hands
and looking up at our beautiful tree
we'll dance and sing
       "Noel Noel"

From "little tree" by E. E. Cummings

*C*hill December brings the sleet,
Blazing fire and Christmas treat.

—Sara Coleridge

*H*eap on more wood!—the wind is chill;
But let it whistle as it will,
We'll keep our Christmas merry still.

—Sir Walter Scott

I once thought that snowflakes were feathers
　　And that they came falling down
When the Moon Lady feathered her chickens
　　And shook out her silver gown.

And then I began to look closer,
　　And now I know just what they are—
I caught one today in my mitten,
　　And there was a baby star.

"Snowflakes" by Marchette Chute

A bundle is a funny thing,
It always sets me wondering . . .
Especially in Christmas week
Temptation is so great to peek!

—John Farrar

Dashing through the snow

In a one-horse open sleigh,

O'er the fields we go

Laughing all the way;

Bells on bobtail ring,

Making spirits bright;

Oh, what fun it is to sing

A sleighing song tonight!

Jingle bells! Jingle bells!

Jingle all the way!

Oh, what fun it is to ride in a one-horse open sleigh!

Jingle bells! Jingle bells!

Jingle all the way!

Oh, what fun it is to ride in a one-horse open sleigh!

From "Jingle Bells" by James Pierpont

When Christmas bells are swinging above the fields of snow,

We hear sweet voices ringing from lands of long ago.

And etched on vacant places,

Are half–forgotten faces

Of friends we used to cherish, and loves we used to know—

When Christmas bells are swinging above the fields of snow.

—Ella Wheeler Wilcox

Your Christmas comes with holly leaves
And snow about your doors and eaves.

—John Runcie

So now is come our joyful feast;
　　let every man be jolly.
Each room with ivy-leaves is dressed,
　　and every post with holly.

—George Wither

Now the bright sun above a brighter world—

A world as white as last month's perfect moon—

Looks all abroad, and on the jeweled trees,

And icicles which taper at the eaves,

Flashes his lavish splendour.

From "New Pastoral" by Thomas Buchanan Reed

'Twas the night before Christmas, when all through the house

Not a creature was stirring, not even a mouse;

The stockings were hung by the chimney with care,

In hopes that St. Nicholas soon would be there.

From "A Visit from St. Nicholas" by Clement C. Moore

The snow lies white on roof and tree,
Frost fairies creep about,
The world's as still as it can be,
And Santa Claus is out.

He's making haste his gifts to leave,
While the stars show his way,
There'll soon be no more Christmas Eve,
Tomorrow's Christmas Day!

—Anonymous

O Children, wake, for a fairy world
  Is waiting for you and me,
With gems aglow on the meadow grass,
  And jewels on every tree.

The hedgerows glitter, the dark woods shine
  In dresses of sparkling white,
For all while we slumbered, the Ice Queen passed
  All over the earth last night.

"A Jewel Day" by Lucy Diamond

We wish you a Merry Christmas;

We wish you a Merry Christmas;

We wish you a Merry Christmas and a Happy New Year!

Good tidings we bring to you and your kin;

Good tidings for Christmas and a Happy New Year!

English Carol

Christmas where snow peaks stand solemn and white,
Christmas where cornfields lie sunny and bright;
Everywhere, everywhere Christmas tonight.

—Phillips Brooks

When as you sing of Christmas cheer
    And welcome in the bright new year,
And feast and laugh and dance and play
    And open gifts on Christmas Day,
Pause as you hear the angel's words,
    And don't neglect the little birds.

—Anonymous

Silent night, holy night,
All is calm, all is bright . . .

Sleep in heavenly peace.
Sleep in heavenly peace.

From"Silent Night"
by Joseph Mohr